Class No. J

Author: HICKEY, To

LEABHARLANN
CHONDAE AN CHABHA

1. **This book may be kept three weeks.**
   It is to be returned on / before the last date
   stamped below.
2. **A fine of 20p will be charged for every week**
   or part of week a book is overdue.

3 MAY 1996		
17 JUL 1996		
19 MAR 1997		
16 JUL 1997		
12 SEP 1997		
12 DEC 1997		
25 MAR 1998		
14 MAY 1998		
8 AUG 1998		
30 OCT 1998		
27 NOV 1998		
14 APR 2000		

TONY HICKEY

Flip 'n' Flop in Kerry

THE CHILDREN'S PRESS

First published in 1995 by
The Children's Press
45 Palmerston Road, Dublin 6

© Text Tony Hickey 1995
© Illustrations The Children's Press

ISBN 0 947962 93 X

Cover Design Maria Murray
Text Illustrations Terry Myler
Typeset by Computertype Limited
Printed by Colour Books Limited

*Dedicated to
the rainmakers of
Streatham*

Contents

Illustrations

1
Saying Good-Bye

It was the day after the wedding of Frank and Lucy. Flip and Flop sat under the big bush at the end of the garden and talked about what a great and exciting day it had been. All afternoon the house and the special tent that had been erected on the terrace had been crowded with laughing, talking, happy people.

Now the tent had been taken away. All the glasses and plates and knives and forks had been collected by the caterers. So too had the folding tables and chairs. In fact there was nothing to indicate that the wedding had ever taken place. It could be the start of just another day. Except, of course, it wasn't – or, at least, not for Flip and Flop. For them, it would be the last morning for a long time when they would sit like this under the big bush and wait for Bella, the dog from next door, to come and talk to them.

When, at last, she did come through the hole in the hedge, she just couldn't help feeling sad. 'I'm going to miss the two of you when you go to live with Frank and Lucy in Kerry,' she said.

'And we will miss you,' said Flip.

'We most certainly will,' agreed Flop.

Then, without really meaning to, the three dogs threw their heads back and keened.

'What a terrible noise!' a very familiar voice said. It was Catriona, the cat, perched on top of the garden wall.

Bella said, 'We're in no mood for any of your clever chat this morning. If you've come around to annoy us, you may just as well buzz off!'

'Dear, oh dear, we *are* feeling sorry for ourselves, aren't we? Most young dogs would be thrilled to be off on a new adventure.'

'And what makes you think it will be an adventure?' asked Flip.

'Because the wise old grey cat, who lives on the hill, told me so,' replied Catriona.

This was not the first time that Catriona had mentioned the wise old grey cat to the dogs. They were not sure whether to believe her or not, although it must be said that, so far, Catriona had never told them a lie. It was just that, in all the times that they had gone for walks on the hill, they had never seen the wise old grey cat.

Then Catriona said, 'I suppose you won't really believe that she exists unless you see her. Well I am proud and happy to tell you that she has come down off the hill specially to speak to you. Come over to the far corner of the garden.'

The three dogs did as Catriona asked. There, sitting in the centre of a clump of shrubs, was a huge dark-grey cat. She nodded to Bella and said, 'Catriona tells me that Flip and Flop are going to live in Kerry.'

'That's right,' said Bella. 'We're feeling a bit sad because of it.'

'Yes, I heard you keening,' said the wise old grey cat. 'It is natural to be sad when leaving friends. It is natural, too, for Flip and Flop to be nervous about the future. That is why I said I would come down and talk to them.' She turned her gaze on the two border terriers. 'I will miss seeing the two of you running across the hill with Bella.'

'We never saw you,' said Flip.

'Oh, I am only seen and heard when I want to be,' the wise old grey cat replied. 'That is why I have been able to live for so long on the hill by myself.'

Flop shivered at the thought of living alone on the hill, especially on dark, mysterious nights like the night that Catriona had taken him and Flip up there. 'Then you don't live with humans at all?' he asked.

'No. When I was a very young kitten I decided I wanted to see as much of Ireland as I could, so I went off on my travels. I spent many happy days in Kerry, which is how I know so much about it. It is one of the nicest, most interesting places in Ireland. People come from all over the world to see it. You are two fortunate young dogs to be able to live there.'

All at once the dogs felt better.

'I have a very good friend down there named Plucky He is an Irish wolf-hound,' continued the wise old grey cat.

'Oh, we know a wolf-hound too,' said Flip. 'We met him at the vet's.'

'They might well be cousins or even grandfather and grandson, for Plucky is almost as old as I am,' said the wise old grey cat

'But not so wise,' Catriona argued.

'Oh yes, he's every bit as wise in spite of being a dog, if I may say such a thing without upsetting anyone,' said the wise old grey cat.

None of the dogs felt at all upset. There was something about the wise old grey cat that made it impossible to be cross with her. Now if Catriona had said such a thing, they would all have been furious!

Catriona wasn't very pleased to hear Plucky being praised by the wise old grey cat. 'I bet he doesn't know as many stories or songs as you do then!' she said. Turning to the dogs, she added, 'The wise old grey cat knows hundreds and hundreds of stories and songs that she learned on her travels. She is teaching them to me so that they won't be forgotten.'

'Plucky in Kerry knows as many stories and songs as I do. His are all about dogs! Flip and Flop must make sure that they meet him. He might even teach them some of his stories.'

'Only of course they won't be very important stories since they are just about dogs,' sneered Catriona.

'Oh, is that so?' snarled Flip.

'Please, please, there is very little time left before Flip and Flop start on their journey. You must not waste any of it quarrelling,' put in the wise old grey cat.

'Quite right,' said Bella. Then suddenly she and the two terriers felt sad again at the thought of there being so little time left!

The wise old grey cat smiled, 'There is no need to feel like that. Catriona, don't tell me you have forgotten about Mr Johnson's surprise!

2

The Surprise

The dogs all stared at Catriona and waited for her to speak. After a long pause, which they knew was meant to annoy them, she said, 'Of course I haven't forgotten about Mr Johnson's surprise. Any moment now he should be back with it.'

'Back from where?' asked Bella. She turned to the terriers. 'Where did Mr Johnson go this morning?'

'Well, first of all he had to take Harry and Joan to catch their train back to school,' said Flip.

'Harry and Joan are the two youngest Johnson children,' Bella quickly explained to the wise old grey cat. 'They were allowed home from boarding-school just for the wedding.'

'And then Mr Johnson was going to drop John and Mary at the airport to catch the plane back to London.'

'John and Mary are married to each other,' Bella told the wise old grey cat. 'John is the eldest of the Johnson children.

He was Frank's best man at the wedding yesterday. But I still don't see where the surprise comes in.'

'You will find out very soon now, if what Catriona has told me is true,' said the wise old grey cat.

'Of course, it's true!' Catriona swished her tail, 'Didn't I hear Mr Johnson talking on the telephone yesterday morning before everyone went rushing off to the wedding?'

'There is no reason to get so excited,' the wise old grey cat said. 'Take things more calmly.'

'I *am* calm,' said Catriona, although she didn't look or sound very calm.

'We might all feel calm if you told us what you heard Mr Johnson say on the telephone,' said Bella. 'I suppose you were outside on the window-ledge, listening as usual.'

'Yes, of course I was,' Catriona admitted proudly. 'That is how we cats find out what's going on.'

'Then, please, tell us now what it was you heard yesterday,' said Flip.

'Well, I heard Mr Johnson saying that he hoped the surprise would be on time. He said that he was going to collect it after he had dropped the children off this morning. He also said that it would be great if it arrived here before the other border terriers went off to Kerry.'

'OTHER BORDER TERRIERS?' Bella repeated the words slowly. 'You are certain that he said the OTHER border terriers?'

'Yes, quite certain,' Catriona said. 'Why do you think that is so important?'

'Because it might mean that...' But, before Bella could finish her sentence, the wise old grey cat held up a paw and said, 'Listen! I think I hear a car coming down the drive. All your questions should be answered in a few minutes.' Then she just slipped away. One second she was there. Next she was gone.

Even Catriona was amazed. Then she heard Mr Johnson getting out of his car and, followed by the dogs, she ran up to the house.

The sliding doors on to the terrace were open. Bella and the terriers went straight into the living-room. Catriona stayed outside on the window-ledge and watched what was happening.

19

Mr Johnson came into the living-room, carrying a big black box. Flip and Flop stared at each other in amazement. The box was just like the one they had travelled in when they had come from Scotland to Ireland. They could hear little snuffling noises coming from inside the box. Bella said 'Mmm. Just as I thought!'

Then Mr Johnson called upstairs to Mrs Johnson, 'Come down, please.'

Mrs Johnson called back, 'I'm helping Frank and Lucy to pack their wedding presents. Can you wait a few minutes?'

'Not really,' Mr Johnson called back. 'This is important. And make Lucy and Frank come down too!'

'Oh, all right so!' Mrs Johnson, Frank and Lucy came downstairs.

Mrs Johnson stared at the box. 'What on earth is that?'

'It is a surprise present for you,' said Mr Johnson. 'In fact it is a present for both of us. The house is going to be very quiet without the children and Flip and Flop. I don't want you to be lonely. And so I bought us these two beauties.'

He stooped down and opened the box.

Out through the door came two little border terrier puppies, who stared around in amazement. Then they saw Flip and Flop and Bella and yelped, 'Where are we? Who are you?'

They tried to run across the polished wooden floor but it was too slippery for them. They skidded and crashed into Bella.

Frank roared with laughter. 'Well you should have no problem naming these two! Call them Slip and Slide.'

That made Lucy and Mr and Mrs Johnson laugh too. Then Mrs Johnson said, 'But are they really ours?'

'Yes, of course, they are! It was all your idea anyway. Do you not remember, after you hurt your leg, that you said you'd like border terriers of your own?' said Mr Johnson. 'I bought them from a kennels in County Clare and had then delivered to the vet's yesterday. He looked after them until I was able to collect them this morning. Are you pleased?'

'I couldn't be more delighted,' said Mrs Johnson. 'And look at Bella! She's delighted as well to have new pups to keep her company.'

Flip and Flop couldn't help feeling jealous at all the attention that Slip and Slide were getting. Then Mr Johnson said, 'But we will always have a soft spot for Flip and Flop, the first border terriers to live in this house.'

Slide said, 'Is that true? Were you the first border terriers to live in this house?'

'We most certainly were,' Flip said proudly. 'And before that we lived in the mountains.'

'And before that, we came to Ireland in a plane all the way from Scotland,' said Flop. 'And now we are going all the way down to Kerry to live.'

'Oh, I hope we have exciting lives like that,' said Slip. 'Will you tell us all about Kerry when we meet again?'

'Of course, we will,' said Flop.

'Try and be good,' advised Flip. 'Do as you are told.'

Catriona laughed mockingly. 'Oh, listen to who is talking.'

'Who's that?' asked Slide.

'That is a cat called Catriona,' said Bella. 'She can be a bit annoying at times.'

'And also very useful when you want to know certain things,' Catriona purred. 'And even though we might not always show it, would you think it very soft of me to say, now that you are leaving, that in our own cat-and-dog way we have become friends?'

'Of course it is not a soft thing to say!' said Bella. 'It is a very good thing to say. I am sure that you and Slip and Slide will become friends too.'

'Yes, I suppose we will,' said Catriona. 'I

wonder if they are brothers or cousins of Flip and Flop?'

All the dogs stared in amazement at the cat, who said, 'Well it stands to reason that, if all wolf-hounds are related in some way, then all border terriers must be related in some way too.'

'But we came from County Clare,' said Slide. 'Flip and Flop came from Scotland.'

'That doesn't mean anything,' said Catriona. 'I know humans whose brothers and sisters live in America. I even know humans with aunts and uncles and cousins who live in places so far away that they have never even met each other.'

'Honestly,' said Mrs Johnson, 'from the way those animals are forever nodding and making noises at each other you would think they were talking to each other.'

'Perhaps they are,' said Frank. 'Perhaps they are saying good-bye to each other.'

'And that is exactly what we should be doing too or we will never get to Kerry before dark,' said Lucy.

Get to Kerry before dark! What a long way away Kerry must be! Flop shivered at the thought of arriving in a strange, new place in the dark! But, before he could say anything to Flip about this, everyone started to hug everyone else and to pet all the dogs and Catriona. Then Flip and Flop were put on the back seat of Frank's car and driven up the drive.

They managed one last glance out of the back window. Mr and Mrs Johnson were standing at the front door waving. They were holding the new pups. Bella was at their feet barking. Catriona was on a window-ledge, waving her tail.

'I wonder how long it will be before we get back to this house,' Flop said sadly.

'Hard to say,' said Flip. 'But it's nice to know that there are still border terriers there.'

'Could they really be our brothers?' asked Flop.

'Maybe Plucky, the wolf-hound, will be able to answer that question,' said Flip.

'Yes, of course,' said Flop. 'I'd forgotten about Plucky for a moment.'

Then he and Flip settled down to enjoy the long journey.

3
To Kerry

At first, looking out through the car windows was very interesting.

Flip and Flop recognised many of the places they were driven past. They saw the vet's house, and the tree at the corner of the road where the woman who clipped their coats lived. Then they went through streets clogged with city centre traffic. Then they left the city far behind and were driven along a fine, straight road through flat, empty fields.

'Where is everyone?' asked Flip. 'They can't all still be in bed.'

'Look over there,' said Flop. 'You can see some mountains. Do you think those are the mountains where we lived with Frank?'

'They probably are,' said Flip. 'Those were very exciting days. I just hope that what the wise old grey cat said about Kerry being a great place is true! Do you think they have sheep in Kerry?'

Both little dogs shivered at the thought

of sheep. Then Flop said, very firmly, 'Even if they do have sheep in Kerry, it has nothing to do with us! We are not allowed to go near sheep.'

After that Flip and Flop fell fast asleep and did not wake until the car stopped.

'Are we there?' Flip asked, sitting up to look out of the window.

'I don't think so,' said Flop. 'It's still bright outside.'

Flop was right. Lucy and Frank had stopped to have something to eat. They also got fresh water and biscuits for the dogs. Then they let them out of the car to do their business.

'They must be afraid we'd be sick in the car if they gave us anything else to eat,' said Flop.

'Well let's hope they give us something decent to eat when we finally get there,' grumbled Flip, settling down for another long snooze.

Flop didn't feel as sleepy as his brother. He sat more or less upright and gazed out of the window. The landscape became more interesting, with hills and lakes and narrow roads to be seen. The car-radio played gentle music so Flop was able to hear what Lucy and Frank were saying. They were planning their lives in Kerry. Frank would make furniture and write his books. Lucy would teach music and acting. It all sounded very interesting. Flop just wished that they had mentioned Plucky, the wolf-hound. Maybe he was like the wise old grey cat on the hill and only let himself be seen and heard when he wanted to be seen and heard.

The car slowed down and stopped again. A wonderful red and orange light came through the windows.

'Oh, just look!' said Lucy.

Flop nudged Flip awake. 'Something's happening,' he said.

The two terriers looked out of the window and saw that the car had stopped on the corner of a hill. There, stretched out in front of them, was the sea but it was quite different from the sea that they were used to seeing from the terrace of the house on the hill where Mr and Mrs Johnson lived.

This sea, with islands scattered here and there, seemed to go on forever. The red

and orange light came from the sun, which was setting behind the mountains overlooking the sea. There were very few houses to be seen and no sign of a town. The only sign of movement were great flocks of sea-birds, returning home after a day's fishing.

It was somehow very lonely and mysterious. Flip and Flop sat closer together. They both shivered slightly.

Frank and Lucy looked at them and smiled. 'Soon be there now,' Frank said cheerfully. 'You deserve a big feed for being so good all through the drive.' But

Flip and Flop didn't really feel very hungry any more.

They felt even less hungry when Frank drove down a narrow, bumpy road where branches of trees slapped against the windows of the car.

The car finally stopped outside a grey, two-storied house. 'Here we are,' said Lucy. 'Home, sweet home.' She opened the car doors and let the dogs out. 'Now, don't you two go running off.'

She had no need to worry about that. Flip and Flop were happy to stay as close as possible to Frank and Lucy as they un-locked the house.

Lucy tried the light-switch in the living-room. Nothing happened.

'A bulb or a fuse must have gone,' she said.

'Perhaps the power hasn't been turned on,' said Frank. 'Did you write and ask the ESB to do it?'

'Yes, I did, or at least I asked my cousin Joe to do it,' said Lucy. 'Perhaps he forgot.'

'He probably did,' said Frank. 'He didn't seem very reliable to me. Still we can manage for one night without electricity.

We have plenty of candles.'

Within minutes the dark cottage was aglow with bright candlelight, and Frank started a fire with some turf stacked by the fireplace. The bottled-gas stove still worked so there was no problem about heating tins of food for supper.

'The beds might be damp,' said Lucy.

'We can use our sleeping-bags down here in front of the fire,' said Frank.

Lucy laughed. 'It is a bit like camping out, only we are doing it indoors.'

And it *was* just like camping out indoors. It was also as though they hadn't

really arrived yet in Kerry, thought Flip and Flop, as they settled down in their basket close to the fire. Maybe it wouldn't all be so dark and gloomy by daylight.

Maybe, too, they would be less worried about something else; when Lucy and Frank had made them go out after supper to do their business, they had been certain that all kinds of creatures had been watching them through the bushes!

A strong wind blew in off the sea. Rain began to bounce off the windows. Then they heard the strangest, keening sound.

'What was that?' Lucy asked sleepily.

'Just a dog, complaining about being left out in the rain,' said Frank.

'Poor thing,' said Lucy and went back to sleep.

So did Frank.

Flip and Flop stayed awake a while longer, thinking of how sad that dog had sounded. Then, in spite of feeling nervous, they too fell asleep and did not wake until the first rays of the morning sun came through the windows and tickled their noses.

4

The Mystery Begins

Frank and Lucy woke at the same time. Lucy immediately went to the front door and opened it wide. 'The storm is over,' she said. 'It's going to be a nice day.'

'But not a very long one,' said Frank. 'Don't forget it will soon be winter. Most people come to Kerry during the summer when the days are long and sunny.'

'Yes, I was forgetting that,' said Lucy. 'I've only ever been here during the warm weather so we had better get moving before the daylight hours are over.'

The daylight hours over! Flip and Flop stared at each other in amazement. Just how short were the days in Kerry going to be?

Suddenly they missed not having Bella or even Catriona to answer their questions. Suddenly they felt very jealous to think that, at that very moment, Slip and Slide were probably sitting under the big bush at the bottom of the garden, being told all kinds of interesting things by Bella and Catriona. Here there didn't even seem to be a garden, just those dark-green bushes growing around the house.

It was in those bushes that Flip and Flop has imagined creatures watching them last night.

But *had* they imagined it? Or had there really been something staring at them? Something watching them even while Lucy and Frank unpacked the car?

In the bright morning light the bushes did not look quite so strange. Flip suddenly had enough of feeling nervous. 'These are our bushes now,' he said to Flop.

There was a scrambling noise in the bushes. A big red and white sheep-dog came into view. 'Hello there, boys,' the dog said. 'My name is Topsy. What's yours?'

'I'm Flip. He's Flop,' Flip said.

Topsy nodded. 'Flip and Flop, eh? Well if they aren't the great names. I'd say now that it is from the city you are with names like that?'

'Well, not exactly from the city,' said Flip. 'We lived just outside Dublin.'

'But we were born in Scotland,' said Flop.

'Oh, so you are very well-travelled for your age,' said Topsy.

'Yes. Where were you born?' asked Flip.

'Just three miles down the road from here,' said Topsy. 'I live with the O'Sullivans.'

'Were you by any chance watching us last night when we arrived?' asked Flop.

'No. I was safe indoors, where any sensible dog should be on a night like that,' replied Topsy. 'Did something upset you?'

'We had a feeling that someone or something was hiding in the bushes around the house,' said Flop. 'And then later on we heard a terrible, keening noise.' He threw back his head and tried to imitate it. 'Who made that noise? You must know all the dogs that live around here. Did you recognise it?'

'I can't be certain what dog it was,' said Topsy, 'but I am on my way to see Jer, who lives with the O'Sheas. He may know.'

Frank came around the side of the house to see what the terriers were doing. 'Oh, so you have visitors already, do you?'

Topsy wagged her tail and allowed Frank to pat her head. Then Frank said to the terriers, 'I'm going to drive into the town to see about having the electricity turned on. You two had better come around to the front door so that Lucy can keep an eye on you. We don't want you wandering off.'

Topsy followed Frank and the terriers. 'Did he say he was going to have the electricity turned on?'

'Yes,' said Flop. 'One of Lucy's cousins was to arrange it but he must have forgotten.'

'No, he didn't forget. The men from the ESB were here the day before yesterday. They made sure it was in working order.'

'Well it didn't work last night,' said Flip.

'Could the storm have broken it?' asked Flop.

'The storm didn't begin until after Lucy tried to turn it on,' said Flip.

'Oh dear, I hope this isn't going to be an adventure like the wise old grey cat on the hill promised us,' said Flop.

'You know the wise old grey cat on the hill, do you?' Topsy was very impressed.

'We met her yesterday morning in the Johnsons' garden. She said we should try and meet Plucky, the wolf-hound,' said Flip. 'Do you know where he is?'

Topsy wrinkled her brow. 'I wish I could answer that question.'

Flip and Flop asked, 'Has he gone to live somewhere else?'

Topsy said, 'That's the problem. He seems to have vanished!'

'How could he vanish?' asked Flip.

Before Topsy could answer, Lucy came out of the house. 'Topsy!' she said. 'You were just a pup last time we saw each other. You and Flip and Flop are going to be great friends. And Frank too, of course.'

'Topsy!' Frank roared with laughter as

he got into the car and drove away. 'What a name for a dog.'

'I just hope he will still be laughing when he finds out about the electricity' said Topsy darkly. 'It was definitely connected by the ESB.'

'Do you think someone deliberately cut it off?' asked Flop, as a great shiver ran down his spine.

'Indeed I do,' said Topsy.' And I can't help feeling that it has something to do with Plucky not being around as usual.'

'Who does Plucky live with?' asked Flip.

'He lives with Jack Foley, but *he* seems to have vanished too,' replied Topsy. 'There's been no sign of him since yesterday.'

The jaws of the border terriers fell open in amazement. Dogs and people didn't just vanish.

'Well, I'd best be off to see if Jer over at the O'Sheas has found out anything,' said Topsy. 'I'll call in on my way back.' She ran off down the road.

5

A Walk By the Sea

Flip and Flop sat in silence for a few seconds. The only sound to be heard was Lucy humming happily as she unpacked the wedding presents and boxes of belongings that she and Frank had brought from Dublin. Then, after a while, she turned on the radio and a woman could be heard singing.

Suddenly Flop didn't care very much for the way Flip was staring at the dark-green bushes around the house. 'What are you thinking about?' he asked.

'I was thinking that maybe we're wasting time just sitting here,' said Flip.

'What else can we do?' asked Flop.

'Maybe we could go exploring,' said Flip. 'Maybe we could find out certain things.'

'Frank and Lucy would be very cross if we went off by ourselves,' warned Flop.

'Only if we got into trouble,' said Flip.'Anyway we could be back before they even miss us. Oh, come on, Flop!

Don't you want to see what this place called Kerry is like? Just sniff the air and tell me what you smell.'

Flop saw no real harm in doing as Flip asked. He took a deep breath. All at once he no longer felt nervous. Instead he felt a great rush of excitement.

'I can smell the sea,' he said. 'And lots of other things as well. It is as if all the smells we have ever known are all here in one place.'

'Yes,' said Flip, 'I feel like that as well. And there is the mystery to solve too. Just think of the great story we would have to tell Bella when we meet her again. She'd be so proud of us.'

'And maybe if we found Plucky, the wolf-hound, he would teach us some of his stories and songs.' Flop was standing up now. His whole body trembled with excitement. The wind blew in off the sea and swept his ears back. 'Maybe it wouldn't do any harm to have a quick look around. But we mustn't go too far.'

'We'll only go as far as the sea,' said Flip. 'We saw it from the car last night so it can't be too far away.'

The two terriers pointed their heads in all directions until they were certain where the smell of the sea was coming from. Then they ran in under the dark-green bushes and out the other side to where there was a wood of tall trees.

Leaves covered the ground and gave the dogs a whole new rush of smells. In spite of being in a hurry, they just had to stop and nose around in the leaves. Some of the smells they recognised from the walks they had gone on with the Johnsons and Bella.

Other smells were completely new to

them. But rather than spend time now trying to follow them, they decided to ask Topsy about them when they next saw her.

Beyond the wood they came to a path. 'This will surely bring us down to the sea,' said Flop. 'Let's follow it.'

And Flop was right. The path wound its way around several huge rocks and ended at the edge of the sea. Instead of the long sandy beach the dogs had been used to, there was a narrow beach of pebbles and great strands of seaweed. A fishing boat bobbed up and down at the end of a rope tied to a rock. The wind that blew across the water made little white waves.

'What do you think?' asked Flip.

'I think it's terrific,' said Flop. 'Sort of exciting.'

'I think that as well,' said Flip. 'I wonder what's around the next corner.' Before Flop could remind him that they had said that they would not go too far, Flip ran off along the water's edge.

Flop decided it was better to go after his brother than let him go off by himself. He had just caught up with him when they heard the same strange, keening noise that they had heard the night before. They tumbled to a stop, banged their heads together and fell down on the pebbles. Flip was first back on his paws. He sniffed the air. Flop stood up and did the same.

Then they listened. They could still hear the keening sound but it was quieter now.

Flop said, 'Something tells me that that is Plucky, the missing wolf-hound. It is almost as though he can only manage to make a loud sound now and again.'

Flip said, 'That is probably because he is very tired calling for help.'

'But where can he be calling from?' asked Flop. 'It can't be from the woods or we'd have got his scent when we walked through them.' He looked around a high rock at the next stretch of pebbles and seaweed. 'And there's no sign of him further on.'

Then he looked across the choppy water. In the middle of the bay there was a tiny island that he hadn't noticed before, with a small hut on it. 'He has to be on that island!'

The two little dogs listened carefully again. Flip said, 'It's hard to be certain with the noise that the wind is making but ... but I think I *do* hear something all right. And it could be coming from that island. We have to get help.'

'Let's go back to our house,' said Flop. 'Maybe we can get Lucy to understand.'

The terriers raced back to the path and up into the woods. They scattered the fallen leaves in all directions and crawled under the dark-green bushes in front of the house. There they came to a standstill. The front door was closed.

'We'd better start barking,' said Flop.

'We should bang and scrape at the door as well, in case Lucy is upstairs,' said Flip.

They did this for several minutes before the terrible thought came to them that the house was empty!

Had Lucy vanished too?

And what about Frank? Would he come back safely from the town? Or would he vanish as well? Would the two dogs end up all alone until it was their turn to vanish?

6

Where's Lucy?

The sound of Topsy calling made them swing around. She was rushing down the narrow road. Behind her was another dog . That had to be Jer, the dog who lived with the O'Sheas.

'What's the matter?' gasped Topsy. 'Why were you making such a noise?'

'You have every dog for miles around barking,' added Jer. 'We thought you were being killed or something.'

'It's Lucy,' cried Flop. 'She's vanished! Flip and I went for a walk and we think we've discovered where Plucky is. We ran back here to try and get Lucy to help us but she's not here.'

Jer said very firmly, 'This thing has gone far enough. Nothing or no one is safe. Where is it you think Plucky is?'

'In that hut on the island in the middle of the bay,' said Flop. 'It's a long way from the land. We would have to go out there in a boat.'

'Oh, so you know about boats, do you?'

'Yes. We went fishing in one with Frank and Bella, our best dog friend,' said Flop. 'But we will need a human to row the one that is tied up down at the beach.'

'That's Jack Foley's boat,' said Topsy.

'First of all we have to find out what has happened to Lucy,' said Flip.

'And we are the two dogs best suited to help you do that,' declared Topsy. 'If Lucy is anywhere to be seen, we will soon know.' Together the two older dogs raised their heads and howled out across the countryside, 'Has anyone seen a human called Lucy?'

Many of the dogs, who until then had just been making barking noises, shouted back, 'What does she look like? What does she look like?'

Before Flip and Flop could answer this question, there was a noise on the roadway and a smell that the terriers had never smelled before.

'It's Mitch!' said Topsy. 'Maybe he has news.'

Flip and Flop rushed forward with Topsy and Jer, expecting to see another dog. Instead they saw a much bigger animal that looked like a long-haired horse! He stared at Flip and Flop.

'What's the matter?' he asked. 'Have you never seen a donkey before?'

'No, we haven't,' replied Flip.

'I suppose that's because you come from the city.' Mitch didn't sound as though he liked dogs from the city.

'They really aren't city dogs,' said Topsy. 'And they've been in a lot of places and know an awful lot of things. They know about boats and fishing.'

Mitch looked more friendly. 'Is that so? Well maybe we will get on together after all.'

'Yes, I'm sure we will,' said Flop. 'Only please, please, have you seen our friend Lucy anywhere?'

'Yes, I think I did. That is if your names are Flip and Flop,' replied Mitch.

'Those are our names all right,' said Flip.

'Well, she has gone off down the road, looking for the two of you,' said Mitch. 'She was calling your names.'

'Oh dear!' said Flop. 'She must have realised that we had gone exploring and got worried. Frank will be furious when

48

he finds out. Let's go after her at once.'

'Let's ALL go after her,' said Flip. 'I have an idea.'

'I'm not sure that this is a good time for one of your ideas,' said Flop. 'We're in enough trouble as it is.'

'That is why we need to do something very, very useful,' said Flip. He turned to Jer and Topsy. 'Could you ask all your friends to start barking again?'

'Yes, of course we can,' said Jer. 'But I would have thought that that would make ALL the humans cross and not just Frank and Lucy.'

'That is what I am hoping will happen,' said Flip. 'And, Mitch, you could help as well, that is if donkeys bark.'

'No, we don't bark. We bray – like this.' Mitch opened his mouth and made the most extraordinary noise that Flip and Flop had ever heard. Almost at once other donkeys from near and far answered him. There was no need for Jer and Topsy to ask their dog friends to join in. They did so as soon as the donkeys began to bray. Then all the other creatures in the area began to call and shout as well.

'Come on, let's catch up with Lucy,' said Flip.

Mitch led the way. The four dogs and the donkey had not gone very far when they saw Lucy standing in the middle of the road. She was listening in amazement to the sounds that the animals, and even some of the birds, were now making. She had to speak loudly so that Flip and Flop could hear her.

She said, 'Oh, so there you are, you bad dogs! I was afraid that you might have got lost! But why are all the animals making such a noise? Is something wrong?'

'Yes,' barked Flip and Flop.

'Yes, yes,' brayed Mitch.

'Yes, yes, yes,' howled Jer and Topsy.

Lucy put her hands over her ears.

'Stop that racket at once,' a gruff voice said. Walking towards them was a grey-haired man, carrying a stick.

'Oh, Mr O'Sullivan,' Lucy said as the dogs and Mitch stopped barking and braying and stepped well away from the stick. 'I don't know what's wrong with them.'

'No more than I know myself,' said Bart O'Sullivan. 'But Topsy never barks without a reason ... What's the matter with you?'

Topsy made a soft keening noise and danced in front of him.

Flip and Flop did the same in front of Lucy, who said, 'I think they are trying to tell us something. I think they want us to follow them.'

'I think you are right,' said Bart. Then he nodded at the animals. 'Lead on so, and we will follow you.'

'This is like the time that we had to get Bella's people to help Mrs Johnson when she fell over the vacuum-cleaner,' Flip said to the other animals as they all hurried back towards the house. 'We will tell you about that sometime if you like.'

'That would be great,' said Mitch. 'What way do we go now?'

'Down to the edge of the sea,' replied Flip.

This was easier said than done as far as the donkey and Bart were concerned. They were much bigger than the dogs and Lucy. They found it hard not to slip and trip but at last they arrived safely at the water's edge.

7

The Mystery Deepens

The countryside was very quiet again.

It was as though everyone and everything were waiting and listening for what was going to happen next.

Topsy dipped a paw in the water, keened and looked at the island. Flip and Flop did the same. Then they looked at the boat.

'There is something on the island that they want us to see,' said Lucy.

The dogs barked softly and wagged their tails.

'Then I had better go and take a look,' said Bart. He hauled the boat in by the rope. 'The oars are here so there's no problem about getting over.'

'Do you want me to come with you?' asked Lucy.

'No, stay here with the animals,' said Bart.

He got into the boat and, in spite of the wind on the water, rowed quickly and easily over to the island. There was a landing-place there for him to tie up the boat. He went at once to the little hut and unbolted the door. As soon as he did, Plucky rushed out.

He licked Bart's hand. Then he saw the dogs and Mitch and Lucy. 'Hello there,' he barked across the bay, 'I thought I'd never be found.'

Plucky's voice was so loud that all the other dogs for miles around began to bark again.

'Stop that,' Bart shouted. 'You will have every man, woman and child in the place driven mad.'

'That's right,' said Flip very softly.

Flop and the others looked at him. All at once they understood what Flip was up to. He wanted all the humans, who heard the noise, to come out of their houses to see what was happening. Maybe that way, whoever had locked Plucky into the hut on the island would come back to make sure that the wolf-hound was still there!

Lucy watched in amazement as Bart lifted the wolf-hound into the boat and rowed back across the bay. 'That's Jack Foley's dog, isn't it?' She caught the end of the rope and held the boat steady while Plucky and Bart got out. 'I remember him well from when I was here on holidays.'

'Yes, Plucky is Jack's dog all right,' replied Bart. 'But who the blazes locked the poor brute up in that hut? He could have starved. And where is Jack? I've just realised that I haven't seen him to-day.'

Jer and Topsy and Plucky and Mitch all thought that Flip was one of the cleverest dogs they had ever met. 'If you hadn't thought of making all the other animals make so much noise, Bart would never have followed us to see what was happening. And Plucky could still be locked up.'

'Ah, yes,' nodded Flip, 'but it was Flop who first said that he thought he could hear Plucky keening in the hut on the island.'

And so both border terriers were praised for being so clever. But there were still very important questions to be answered.

Flop asked the first question, as the animals and the humans went back to the house: How was it that neither Jer nor Topsy guessed that Plucky was on the island?

'It could have been because of the wind blowing in off the sea,' said Jer. 'It makes it difficult to know exactly where a sound is coming from. And, of course, it would not have occurred to us that Plucky could be on the island.'

'We might never have guessed that either if we hadn't gone exploring,' said Flip.

'But who put you out there?' Mitch asked Plucky.

'Two strangers, humans that I never saw before,' said Plucky. 'They were in a car.'

'I think I hear a car now,' said Mitch.

'Maybe they've come back.'

But the car that was stopping in front of the house belonged to Frank. He stared at all the animals and at Bart O'Sullivan. 'What's happening here, then?'

When he heard the story he was even more amazed. 'And I,' he said, 'have something interesting to tell you too. It seems that the electricity was turned on in the house for us. But before we arrived someone cut it off.'

'If only they could understand what we are saying,' said Plucky.' I could tell them about the strangers in the car.'

'I was sure that all the noise that we and the others made would have brought the strangers down here to see what was happening,' said Flip. 'But that doesn't seem to have worked.'

'That's because of all the other humans still around,' said Topsy. 'Funny how they are always here when you don't need them.'

'Maybe they will go away soon,' said Flop.

And that was what happened when Bart said to Lucy and Frank, 'I suppose the ESB will be around to fix things. It might save a bit of time if we were to go and look for the place where the electricity was cut off.'

'Interfering with the electricity supply is such a stupid, not to mention a dangerous, thing to do,' said Frank as he and Lucy followed Bart down the narrow road. 'Why would anyone want to do such a thing?'

'To make you feel unwelcome would be my guess,' said Bart 'Or maybe to frighten you away. Cutting the electricity might be just the first of many things that were due to happen.'

This piece of news made the dogs stare silently at each other for several seconds. But as soon as Bart and Frank and Lucy had gone from view, they all began to talk at once. Plucky held up a paw for silence. 'Now, now, now,' he said. 'Let's have less noise or those strangers will never come near the place. Let us find places to hide and see what happens next.'

8
The Strangers

Flip and Flop shivered with excitement as they slipped under the dark-green bushes close to the house.

Plucky hid between the trees on the edge of the wood. Jer jumped down into the damp ditch by Frank's car. From there he could see up and down the narrow road. Topsy decided that the best place for her was behind a great clump of brown bracken, next to the footpath to the O'Sullivan farm. Mitch moved into a rocky field and pretended to be grazing.

That way they were able to watch all the ways of getting to the house.

Away in the distance they could hear Bart talking. Everything else seemed to be as it should be.

'Maybe the strangers won't come back,' Flop whispered hopefully to Flip. All this excitement was becoming too much for him.

Then it was no longer possible to hear Bart's voice. He and Frank and Lucy must have gone as far as the main road to look for the damaged electric wires.

Suddenly Mitch brayed softly. 'There are two people coming across the next field. It looks to me as though they are heading for this place.'

Plucky said, 'No one is to move until I get a good look at them. We have to find out what they are up to.'

The next few minutes seemed to go on forever. Then at last the dogs could hear the two humans talking. One was a man. The other was a woman.

It was the woman's voice they heard first. She said, 'I don't like the way things are going, Jake. Why were all the animals making such a noise?'

'Because that is something that animals do, especially dogs,' replied Jake. 'When one of them barks, they all have to bark. They are just stupid.'

Somehow Flip and Flop managed not to growl at this.

'They are not the only stupid things! Cutting off the electricity here was a terrible idea,' said the woman. 'Why should that scare them away? They probably thought it was a breakdown.'

'If I had had time to block the chimney and make the fireplace smoke, they'd have left quickly enough. They just got here sooner than I expected,' said Jake.

From where they lay under the bushes, Flip and Flop could now see the two strangers. The woman had dark hair that peeped out from under a knitted hat. The man had on a peaked cap. They both wore dark jackets and jeans. They paused at Frank's car, then glanced down the road.

'Maureen,' said Jake, 'Maybe you should stay as look-out in case they come back'

'No, thanks!' she replied. 'If they saw me they could describe me to the guards.'

'Oh, all right then,' he said crossly. 'Then you'd better let the front tyres of this car down.'

'What good will that do?'

'It will stop them from being able to drive after us if we have to make a run for our own car down on the main road. Now just do it.'

Jake went into the house. Maureen sighed and begin to let down the car tyres.

Flip and Flop got ready to rush out,

barking, from under the bushes But there was no signal from Plucky. Nor was there any sign of Bart O'Sullivan and Frank and Lucy coming back.

Jake came out of the house with Frank's brief-case. 'Look what I found,' he said with a nasty grin. 'It seems that we have a writer living in this place.'

'And what has that got to do with anything?' Maureen asked as she brushed mud off her hands.

'Everything,' he grinned. 'Unless I'm very much mistaken, I have all the writer's floppy discs and notes for his work in this brief-case. I think he will do whatever we tell him to do and that includes minding his own business'

Flip and Flop had never heard such a wicked idea. This stranger was going to force Lucy and Frank to do as he said, otherwise he would destroy months and months of Frank's work. Oh why, oh why, didn't Plucky give them the signal to rush out and give the two stranger a terrible fright? They could also warn Lucy and Frank and Bart O'Sullivan.

'Now to see to the mutt,' said Jake.

'The mutt? What did he mean by "the mutt"?'

The two strangers passed within inches of Flip and Flop and headed towards the wood. Plucky stood so still between the trees that he seemed to become one of them. But, as soon as the strangers had reached the path down to the beach, he moved into the open and nodded to the other dogs to join him. 'We must go on being very quiet,' he whispered.

'Jake said they were going to see to "the mutt". What's the mutt?' asked Flip.

Plucky said, 'I'm afraid they mean me

when they say "the mutt". It is a way some humans, who think that we are stupid, have of speaking about dogs. And in case you think that I must have been very stupid to let them lock me in the hut on the island, let me just say that you will have to wait until you hear the full story later on.'

The other dogs nodded in agreement and followed the two strangers. Because of the leaves on the ground, the dogs made no sound at all. They were able to reach the bend in the path and listen to what the strangers were saying without being noticed.

Maureen pointed to the hut on the island. 'The door is wide open! The mutt is gone! Someone has rescued him. You don't think it could have been old Foley, do you?'

'Not unless someone has rescued *him* first,' said Jake. 'We'd better go and see.'

'We might be best to just clear out altogether.' Maureen sounded frightened.

'We can't do that,' replied the man. 'Supposing old Foley is still tied up where we left him? It might be days and days before anyone found him. We could end up in worse trouble if he got sick and, maybe, even died. Let's go and check on him right now.'

The dogs quickly slipped back in among the trees as the two strangers hurried back up the path to the house. Here Jake paused and looked at Frank's car. 'Pity we let the tyres down. We could have saved a lot of time by borrowing it now instead of having to go back across the fields.'

'Well I'm not going back across any more fields. I want to stay on the road – not that it's much of a road. We should never have come here in the first place,' Maureen snapped back. 'It's all too wild and lonely for my liking. And I feel as though we are being watched all the time. Look at that donkey there. He hasn't taken his eyes off us for a second.'

'Don't be so stupid,' Jake said. 'He's just looking at us because there is nothing else to look at.'

'That's what you think,' Mitch whispered as he watched the strangers hurry down the narrow road.

9
The Chase

They had not gone very far when they met Lucy, Frank and Bart O'Sullivan, who prevented them from passing.

'Who are you?' he asked 'Where have you come from?'

'We were out for a walk and got lost,' said Jake. 'We thought this way might bring us back to the main road.'

'And so it will,' said Bart. 'But where is it you are coming from?'

'Oh, just from back there,' Jake said. 'Anyway it's a free country. We can walk where we want.'

'Indeed and you can not!' said Bart. 'It's all private property back there. I don't suppose you would know anything about certain electric wires being cut?'

'And that happens to be my brief-case that you have,' said Frank. 'Where did you get if from?' He snatched it back.

'Just what are you up to?' demanded Bart.

Instead of answering, Jake pushed him

backwards towards the ditch. Frank and Lucy tried to save him from falling, and all three slipped on the soft damp ground. The two strangers ran as fast as they could towards the main road. Mitch kept up with them on his side of the hedge and watched as they reached the main road, where their car was parked. They clambered into the car and drove off so quickly that it almost skidded out of control!

At that moment Plucky and the other dogs caught up with Mitch, who said, 'They've gone off in a car!'

Topsy said, 'We'll never be able to keep up with a car.'

'We don't have to keep up with it,' said Flop. 'All we have to do is watch where it is going. Mitch can easily see over the walls and the hedges. The strangers can't be going too far if they arrived here so soon after all the animals made all that noise.'

'That's very true,' said Plucky. 'And I can see over the walls and some of the hedges as well.'

'We could all see if we climbed up,' declared Topsy.

Jer and Topsy had no trouble getting on

top of the wall but Flip and Flop needed a push up from Mitch. Then they were all able to see the strangers' car as it travelled up the side of the nearest mountain.

'I bet I know where they are going,' said Plucky. 'They are going to the cave of O'Donoghue the Brave! We must get there too as quickly as we can.'

'The quickest way is across the fields,' said Flip.

'Exactly!' said Plucky.' I think you two dogs are among the cleverest I've ever known.'

Flip and Flop exchanged delighted looks but that was all they had time to do before they jumped down off the wall and started off towards the mountains.

Mitch and Plucky and the other two dogs knew every gap in every hedge and every short cut through every farmyard. Many other dogs ran alongside them for a while, asking where they were going.

Plucky just replied, 'We will tell you everything later on. But, please, no barking of any kind right now! We are trying to surprise a couple of hostile humans.'

But of course other humans didn't

understand what Plucky was saying. Before very long several of them, including Paddy and Sheila O'Shea, with whom Jer lived, were running after the donkey and the dogs.

Fortunately the O'Sheas were fit young people who didn't smoke and so they soon caught up with the animals.

'I wonder what's got into them at all!' said Paddy.

'Well, whatever it is, isn't it a great bit of

69

excitement?' laughed Sheila, as she scrambled through the last hedge and out on to the mountain road.

From there it was just a short way to the cave of O'Donoghue the Brave but, even as the cave came into view, the strangers rushed out of it and jumped into their car.

But before they could drive away, all the animals and the humans rushed forward and formed a circle.

Jake got out and raised his hands. 'OK, OK,' he scowled. 'We give up.'

'But what is it you were doing that made all these animals rush after you?' asked Paddy.

The animals provided the answer by rushing into the cave and making as much noise as possible. The O'Sheas, leaving the other humans to watch the strangers, followed, and gasped in amazement when they saw Jack Foley, bound and gagged, in a corner of the cave.

As soon as they had untied him he said, 'Thanks be to God that you got here!'

'It was the dogs and the donkey that led us here,' said Paddy. 'Otherwise we might never have known what was going on. In fact, even now, we don't know what's going on.'

'I will tell you everything as soon as I get a bit of warmth into my bones, for I am as cold as can be from being held prisoner in this place,' replied Jack.

'What you need is a cup of hot tea and something to eat,' said Sheila. 'Those two strangers outside can do something useful for a change and drive us all back to our place.'

'What about the animals?' asked Paddy.

'Oh, they'll have no trouble finding their way back to where they came from,' said Jack. He bent down and gave Plucky a big hug and a pat. 'I'm glad that you are all right.' Then he noticed Flip and Flop. 'And who are these two lads then?'

'I think they belong to Lucy and her husband Frank,' said Sheila.

'Well, you are very welcome to Kerry,' said Jack. 'I've a feeling that the two of you and the other dogs are going to be great friends.'

As you can imagine, Flip and Flop now felt so happy and proud with all the attention and praise that they had received that morning that it was as much as they could do not to go running and barking around the cave. But, somehow, they managed not to do this.

Instead they walked slowly along with the others. And, as they walked along, Plucky told them the full story of what had been happening over the last couple of days.

10
Plucky's Story

'It all began two days ago,' said Plucky, 'when Jack Foley and I were walking through the woods at the back of Flip and Flop's house and heard voices coming from the house. We knew that the electricity was due to be reconnected, so we thought that it was the ESB people who were there. Jack thought it might be nice to say 'hello' to them. But when we got to the front of the house there was no sign of anyone. There wasn't even an ESB van to be seen.'

Flip and Flop could picture Jack Foley and Plucky outside the house, looking very puzzled, while the two strangers watched them through the dark-green bushes that grew so close to the house.

'Then Jack noticed that the front door was open. He thought that maybe the ESB people were finishing up some work in the kitchen and had left their van parked down on the main road. But, as he went inside the house, I suddenly got the scent of the strangers. Before I could manage even the smallest growl the man that we were chasing just now appeared as if out of nowhere and caught me by the throat.'

'He and the woman were hiding in the bushes,' Flip said. 'They were there last night watching us. We could sense them but there were too many new smells for us to know what they were.'

'That's right,' said Flop. 'And the lights weren't working. And there was the storm. It was all very creepy.' He shivered as he remembered. Then he thought of how

Plucky must have felt when the man grabbed him. 'You must have been very frightened.'

'I wasn't just frightened,' Plucky said, 'I was also very cross with myself. After all, I'm a wolf-hound. Wolf-hounds are supposed to be able to smell and see things before they happen.'

'Now, now, don't go blaming yourself,' said Jer. 'Even the best of us can make a mistake now and again That's a well-known fact.'

'All the same, it just shouldn't have happened,' said Plucky.

'The man must have been very strong to be able to hold you like that,' Flop said, hoping that this might make Plucky feel better.

'It wasn't that he was so strong,' replied Plucky. 'It was more the kind of grip that he had me in. I felt as though I might choke if I tried to get out of it. But all the same I must have managed to make some kind of noise because Jack came rushing back out of the house. You should have seen his face when he saw what was going on! "Who are you?" he asked. "And what are you doing to that dog?" But the man still held me as tightly as ever.'

The animals had reached the gap from the mountain road into the first of the fields. They started slowly across it, all the time listening to Plucky.

'Indeed if anything the man tightened this grip on me and said, "I won't let go of him until you tell us where the money is!" As you can imagine Jack was even more amazed when he heard this. "What money?" he asked. "I don't know anything about any money." But the strangers didn't believe him."

'I wonder what gave them the idea that Jack Foley had any money in the first place,' puzzled Topsy.

'They didn't think *he* had the money. It was all on account of a story that they had heard in a pub in the town,' said Plucky. 'They stopped in for a drink on their way somewhere else. Someone in the pub was telling a story about a great pile of money being found in a house in Galway. The strangers were very interested in the story.'

'Humans are always interested in stories about money,' said Jer. 'That's another well-known fact that I've noticed for certain over the years!'

'Another thing you may have noticed is that there are some humans who can't stand not to tell a story that's better than the one someone else has just told,' said Plucky.

The two older dogs and the donkey nodded in agreement.

'Well, as luck would have it, who was in the bar listening to the story about the money being found in Galway but old Matt, who lives up by the lake,' continued Plucky.

'A terrible man,' sighed Topsy. 'Always making things up.'

'He's famous for it,' declared Mitch.

'Not that he means any harm,' said Plucky. 'And most humans who know him don't pay much attention to him'

'But the two strangers did?' said Flip.

'Exactly right,' said Plucky. 'They didn't know that he was just looking for attention.'

The animals were now in the next field. The clouds had vanished from the sky. The countryside and the mountains looked clear and clean and fresh. The sea could be seen sparkling under the bright autumn sunlight.

'What old Matt told the strangers was that many people around here were convinced that there was an even bigger pile of money hidden in a house close to the wood overlooking the sea. He also said that the house had been empty this long time but that two people from Dublin would be moving into it very soon.'

'He was talking about our house!' exclaimed Flip.

'Well, he didn't actually name it but it

certainly sounded like your house,' said Plucky. 'That was why the strangers came to it in search of the money. But they couldn't start to look for it right away because the ESB workers were there during the day.'

'Could they not have looked for it at night?' asked Flip.

'No. They would have had to use a flashlight and someone might have noticed it,' replied Plucky. 'So they just had to wait until they were sure that the ESB workers were finished. The morning that Jack and I met them was the first real chance that they had to search the house. And they thought that Jack was looking for the money too.'

The other animals sensed that Plucky was getting to an even more exciting part of his story. They stopped walking and stood around the wolf-hound.

'Being strangers to the place they didn't know who he was. But even when he told them that he owned all the land around the house and that old Matt had made the whole thing up, they still didn't believe him.'

'Or perhaps they just didn't want to believe him,' said Mitch, as he leaned over and tugged at a nice clump of withered thistles.

'Yes, often it is hard to admit that you have been made a fool of. So the strangers decided that the reason why Jack had never looked for the money before this was because he, too, had only just heard old Matt's story. They said that he was trying to get rid of them so that he could start looking for the money himself.'

'And did the man have you by the throat all this time?' asked Flop.

'Yes, he did. I could see how upset Jack was getting. He's very fond of me, you know.'

'We are all very fond of you,' Topsy said gently.

'And I am very fond of all of you,' the wolf-hound replied. Then, as he continued his story, he became very serious again. 'And so the strangers had a problem, which was how to prevent Jack from going to the guards. They had to get him out of the way while they searched the house. And they couldn't leave me with him in case I barked. That would have brought people around to investigate.'

'And it was then that the strangers thought of the hut on the island,' said Flip.

'Now you have it to perfection,' said Plucky. 'They tied up Jack and left him in the house. Then they dragged me through the woods and down to the beach. They must have noticed the boat and the island when they were snooping around earlier on. I've never felt so helpless as when they bundled me into that boat. Maybe it's a sign that I am growing old but I just didn't seem to be able to struggle.'

'It could also be because of the fright you'd had earlier when the man grabbed you,' said Jer. 'It's a well-known fact that a fright can leave you very tired in the long run.'

Topsy and Mitch nodded their heads in agreement. Flip and Flop did the same, although they had never before heard that getting a fright could make you tired.

'Well anyway they rowed across to the island, pushed me inside the hut and locked the door,' said Plucky. 'Then they must have come back, collected their car and taken Jack up to the cave.'

'Was that not a risky place to leave him?' asked Mitch. 'A lot of visitors go there.'

'Not at this time of the year,' replied Plucky. 'So there wouldn't be any risk from them. The humans around would have thought that a strange car just meant a few late tourists. And don't forget that they only meant to leave Jack there for a very short time. The change of plan was caused by these two lads arriving with Frank and Lucy.'

'That must have been when they cut off the electricity to the house!' Flip and Flop both quivered with excitement at the thought that the strangers had been watching them all the time. 'They were even planning to block the chimney and smoke us out. It was a good thing that they didn't get time to do that. There were enough candles to manage without the electricity but we'd never have been able to put up with the house filled with smoke.'

'Smoke can be very dangerous,' said Jer. 'That's another well-known fact.'

All the animals nodded their heads again.

'But go on with the story,' urged Topsy. 'Why didn't you bark as soon as they left you in the hut?'

'I was afraid of what might happen to Jack. Don't forget that I didn't know where they had taken him. And I suppose the same thing was true of him. If he had managed to get away, he'd have been afraid of what might happen to me if he said anything to the guards.'

'But we heard you keening. So did Topsy. That's how we knew where you were,' said Flip.

'Yes, I did keen a few times. I felt very alone and cold and hungry, and worried too, of course.' The wolf-hound raised his head and sighed sadly.

'But all's well that ends well,' said Jer. 'That's another well-known fact.'

'Of course it is,' shouted Topsy. 'And it really is thanks to Flip and Flop that things have worked out so well.'

Flip and Flop again felt as though they would burst with happiness. And yet they felt that they couldn't take all the credit for what had happened.

'Oh no! Please,' they said, 'we only did

what had to be done'

Plucky laughed a deep doggie laugh. 'Is it shy that you are at being praised? Well maybe that is not a bad thing in young dogs.'

'It most certainly is not a bad thing in young dogs. A bit of shyness in young dogs is a GOOD thing,' said Jer. 'And that's another well-known fact. But now maybe it's time we all went back to my place to see what's going on there.'

'And I will lead the way,' Mitch shouted.

Suddenly they were all running as fast as they could. Even Plucky forgot how tired he felt as he and the other dogs followed the donkey across the fields and through the hedges.

Flip and Flop barked and barked and barked. So too did Topsy and Jer, while Mitch kicked up his heels and brayed as loudly as he possibly could. By the time they reached the O'Shea farmhouse, every animal for miles around was answering them back.

'Heavens above, what's got into them at all?' Sheila asked as the dogs looked into the kitchen. Jack Foley was sitting by the

fire with a mug of hot, sweet tea in his hands. He was already feeling much better.

The two strangers sat sulking by the window. The guards would soon be along to take them away! There was a dish of food on the floor for Plucky.

'The poor brute must be starving,' Paddy O'Shea said.

'I'd say Jer could do with a small snack

as well,' suggested Jack.

Suddenly Topsy and Flip and Flop felt very hungry too. It was also time they got back to their house to see how Lucy and Frank and Bart O'Sullivan were.

'We'll see you later on,' they said to Jer and Plucky.

'You surely will,' Plucky said between mouthfuls. 'Safe home!'

11
All Friends Together

Mitch led the three dogs across the last field before the wood and the house. He could see over the hedge as they walked along. 'Lucy and Frank are tying to fix the flat tyres on the car,' he said. 'They don't look very pleased!'

And indeed Lucy and Frank were not very pleased. They could be best described as being downright cross. They were particularly cross with Flip and Flop.

'How dare you run off like that again! Twice in the one day,' said Lucy.

'Just you wait until we've finished with these tyres and you'll get a good whacking with a newspaper!' Frank had managed to put the spare tyre on the car and was now trying to pump up one of the flat tyres with a foot-pump.

He and Lucy were covered in mud. 'That must be from falling over when they tried to save Bart O'Sullivan,' said Flop.

Lucy pushed her hair back off her face. 'Go into the house and be quiet.'

The three dogs slunk into the house, thinking how unfair it was that humans couldn't understand simple dog-talk. Bart O'Sullivan was sitting by the table. His left foot was propped up on a stool.

'Oh, so the wanderers have returned, have they? I don't know much about Flip and Flop but I must say that I was very surprised by you, Topsy, at the way you ran off at the first sign of trouble.'

'At the first sign of trouble? Me run away at the first sign of trouble?'

Topsy was so indignant that she could hardly speak.

The two terriers felt exactly the same way. 'But how can we make them understand that we rushed off so as to rescue Jack Foley and not because we were afraid?'

Bart O'Sullivan moved his left foot and gasped with pain. 'I just wish I could get my hands on those two strangers. I'm sure that I've sprained my ankle from being pushed into the ditch. They are probably miles away by now.'

'No, they're not,' the three dogs started to say together. 'They've been caught! They are over at the O'Sheas!'

Lucy and Frank came angrily into the house. Frank said, 'I thought you were told not to make any more noise. Now stop it!'

Flip and Flop had never heard Frank sound so angry. They decided the best thing to do was to crawl under the table until he was in a better mood. Topsy crawled in beside them.

'The tyres seem OK now. As soon as we've washed our hands, we'll go straight into the town and tell the guards what has happened,' Frank said

'I wonder why they didn't use Bart's car?' Topsy whispered.

'Maybe because Bart couldn't walk to his house on his hurt ankle. Lucy and Frank might have been afraid to leave him here by himself in case the strangers returned,' Flop whispered back.

Lucy looked under the table at the three dogs. 'I hope you are sorry for what you've done.'

'But we've done nothing wrong,' whimpered Flop.

Lucy suddenly smiled as though she had understood what he had said. 'Oh, but

you are such nice little dogs. I don't really
have the heart to be cross with you. Or
with you either, Topsy!'

'You will only spoil them if you go on
like that,' said Frank. All the same when
he looked under the table, he couldn't help
but smile at the sight of the two border
terriers and Topsy all huddled together.

Then there was the sound of a car
coming along the narrow road. Topsy and
the terriers rushed out from under the
table and through the front door like
arrows from a bow! No one would ever
again would be able to think that they ran
off whenever trouble appeared!

But far from being trouble, the people in
the car were Paddy and Sheila O'Shea,

with Jack and Plucky in the back seat.

'We just thought we'd drop in and tell you what all the excitement was about,' said Sheila. 'And the great part that Topsy and your two little dogs played in it.'

The humans all sat around the kitchen table, with the four dogs at their feet. Jack Foley told the same story that Plucky had about being kidnapped by the two strangers, Jake and Maureen. Then the O'Sheas filled in the details of how the dogs and the donkey had led them to the cave!

More praise was then given to the dogs and especially to Flip and Flop. Flip said to Flop, 'I wish there was some way that we could let Bella know what a great adventure we've had!'

Flip had no sooner spoken than his wish came true, for Frank said, 'Wait until I tell Mum and Dad about what has just happened! I said I'd telephone to let them know that we had arrived safely. Maybe we should do that when we take Bart to the doctor to have his ankle seen to.'

'That's a great idea,' said Lucy. 'I'd come with you if I thought the dogs could be left alone.'

'I'll gladly stay and keep an eye on them until you all get back,' said Jack.

'Are you sure you feel strong enough after what's happened to you?' asked Lucy.

'It would take more than a couple of days in a cave to get a Kerryman down,' said Jack. 'And, anyway, aren't the two strangers in garda custody now? We have nothing more to fear from them, although I think they are more stupid than wicked.'

And so the O'Sheas went back to their place, while Lucy and Frank drove Bart into the town, and Jack took it nice and easy in front of the fire.

The dogs went outside and lay in the sunshine. 'It would have been nice if they'd given us something to eat,' said Topsy.

'Don't worry. They will when they come back,' said Plucky. 'Humans sometimes forget things when they are in a hurry.'

'And that's a well-known fact!' For a second it sounded as though Jer was back with them, but it turned out to be Mitch, leaning over the hedge.

'You sounded just like him,' Flip said.

'It reminds me of the story of the donkey that could sing opera,' said Plucky. 'Did I 'ever tell you that one?'

The other animals all shook their heads.

'I first heard it from the wise old grey cat that used to come visit Kerry a long time ago,' said Plucky.

'She lives on a hill near the Johnsons,' Flip said. 'We know her. She said you were one of the best story-tellers in Ireland.'

'That's praise indeed,' said Plucky.

'She also said that you might be related to the wolf-hound that we met at the vet's.'

'That could well be true,' said Plucky.

'Then we might be brothers of Slip and Slide, the new border terriers at the Johnsons,' said Flop.

'That's right. Just as one day the two of you might be famous all over Ireland for what happened here to day,' said Plucky.

'You mean you might put us in a story?' gasped Flip.

'I might,' said Plucky.

'Frank is going to put us in a story as well,' said Flop. 'He said that a long time ago.'

'Then you really will be famous,' said Topsy.

'And so will you,' said Flip. 'And Jer

and Mitch.'

'Hee-haw,' brayed the delighted Mitch. 'But now I want to hear the story about the donkey that could sing opera...'

While Plucky told them the story of the donkey that could sing opera, Flip and Flop couldn't help picturing, even as they listened, the house on the hill and what would happen there in a few minutes' time.

The telephone would ring. Mrs Johnson would answer it. She would be delighted to hear from Frank and Lucy. Then they would tell her all about the adventure with the strangers.

When Mr Johnson came into lunch she would repeat the story to him.

All the time Catriona would be sitting on a window-ledge, listening. She would tell the story to Bella and Slip and Slide, who would be very impressed. And perhaps they would wish that they could come and visit Flip and Flop in Kerry!

And who's knows but they might do that very thing when winter was over!

TONY HICKEY is one of Ireland's leading authors for children. This is his eleventh book for The Children's Press. the others are:

The Matchless Mice
The Matchless Mice's Adventure
The Matchless Mice in Space
The Matchless Mice's Space Project
The Black Dog
Flip 'n' Flop
More About Flip 'n' Flop
Adventures with Flip 'n' Flop
The Castle of Dreams
The Glass Globe Adventure

He is a founder-member of the Irish Children's Book Trust, and a co-founder of The Children's Press.

The Glass Globe Adventure

First problem is that it seems everyone
– Kate and Rory, Brigid and Sam –
wants the glass globe that hangs in
Mrs Foley's window. That solved,
problem number two is good old dosh.
Can the friendly four raise it?
And by the deadline of Christmas Eve?
More problems, involving cars, carols, turkeys
and some distinctly unfriendly adults.
Then just as everything seems about to come
right, the glass globe disappears …

128pp   **£2.95**